ESCAPE FROM YOKAI LAND

ALSO BY CHARLES STROSS

Singularity Sky

Iron Sunrise

Accelerando

Glasshouse

Halting State

Saturn's Children

Rule 34

Scratch Monkey

The Rapture of the Nerds
(with Cory Doctorow)

Neptune's Brood

THE MERCHANT PRINCES

The Bloodline Feud
(comprising *The Family Trade*
and *The Hidden Family*)

The Traders' War
(comprising *The Clan Corporate*
and *The Merchants' War*)

The Revolution Trade
(comprising *The Revolution Business*
and *The Trade of Queens*)

Empire Games

Dark State

CHARLES STROSS

▶◀▶◀▶◀▶◀▶◀▶◀▶◀▶◀▶◀

ESCAPE FROM YOKAI LAND

A TOM DOHERTY ASSOCIATES BOOK
NEW YORK

ESCAPE FROM YOKAI LAND

Copyright © 2021 by Charles Stross

All rights reserved.

Edited by Teresa Nielsen Hayden

A Tordotcom Book
Published by Tom Doherty Associates
120 Broadway
New York, NY 10271

www.tor.com

Tor® is a registered trademark of
Macmillan Publishing Group, LLC.

The Library of Congress Cataloging-in-Publication Data
is available upon request.

ISBN 978-1-250-80570-6 (hardcover)
ISBN 978-1-250-80571-3 (ebook)

Our books may be purchased in bulk for promotional,
educational, or business use. Please contact your local bookseller
or the Macmillan Corporate and Premium Sales Department
at 1-800-221-7945, extension 5442, or by email at
MacmillanSpecialMarkets@macmillan.com.

First Edition: March 2022

Printed in the United States of America

0 9 8 7 6 5 4 3 2 1

For Andrew, Tomiko, and Hana

ESCAPE FROM YOKAI LAND

"I'm sorry, Bob," says Dr. Armstrong, "but they asked for you *specifically* because Hello Kitty is a Londoner."

It's a Friday afternoon in May, and I'm making a futile attempt to get out of the most pointless waste of time and energy to land on my desk this year. I tried Mrs. MacDougal in HR first, but she just sneered at me and told me to man up. (Few people ever win a face-off with Emma; decades of disciplining idiots who send dick-pics from work—or ovipositor pics, in some cases—have turned her heart to granite.) So, after getting knocked back by HR, I went to lobby the Senior Auditor. He has a better grasp of what this kind of liaison job entails than HR—he's been there himself, after all. But I'm getting an unexpectedly unsympathetic hearing.

"What part of 'our eighth wedding anniversary' isn't getting through to you? Mo will assume I forgot, and blame me. You know that thing she does, when she turns so chilly that her sense of irony achieves superconductivity? I'm talking *freezer burns.* And that's before we get into my four-month-deep to-do list of Severity One containment issues that need my official attention, *stat,* because—" I stop. My old boss, Angleton, isn't here anymore, and I'm working my way through his backlog of jobs and it kind of sucks, but I'm not placing any blame on his shoulders. "I don't *need* this right now," I continue, and even to my own ears it comes out a little petulant.

"Bob." Dr Armstrong gives me a long-suffering look. "You're *separated.*"

"Not through choice! And in any case there are loads of high-priority jobs on our doorstep, stuff we're officially tasked with locking down right here without buggering off on a foreign assistance junket. I still haven't finished decontaminating Gruinard"—(the press think it's anthrax spores: if they had any inkling what Churchill ordered tested there during the war it'd trigger a mass panic)—"and then there's the thing in Shaft Ten at Dounreay, not to mention the anomalous readings near Malham Cove—"

"Enough!" Dr. Armstrong eyes me like a university professor sizing up a student who's spending more time in the bar than the library. "They wouldn't be asking for you without a very good reason. James was there in '46, and again in '77. They're due another visit round about now anyway, you're his direct successor, and it *is* our responsibility. Postwar UN occupation, residual cleanup per international treaty. You can't let this slide, it'll make us look shifty and unreliable. *More* shifty and unreliable," he corrects himself, clearly thinking of our beloved coalition government and their attitude toward foreign aid (encouraged when it's a fig leaf for defense industry exports; otherwise, not).

He straightens up and proceeds to hand down judgment. "You need to go to Japan to check the hit list of warded sites James left behind in case any of them are leaking. You need to look into this business in— where is it, Tama New Town?—that our colleagues from the Miyamoto Group are banging on about. Explain what happened to Dr. Angleton and introduce yourself as his successor, then bring them up to date on recent developments. While you're at it you should read, digest, and apply the guidelines in chapters eight through eleven of the *Civil Service Overseas Liaison Handbook* while bearing in mind best practices for

Foreign Office adjuncts on temporary posting over-seas."

"Crap." I surrender to the inevitable as he opens a drawer in his desk and rummages furiously for a few seconds. "Can I just say—"

"Here you are! A local travel guide: James swore by it." He pushes a dog-eared paperback at me—*The Book of Yokai: Mysterious Creatures of Japanese Folklore.* "I think you might find it amusing. I'll talk to Mrs. MacDougal about clearing your travel and expenses authorization in case it exceeds your discretionary budget cap—Land of the Rising Yen, ha ha—and see if she can sort out a diplomatic visa. You'll need to be assigned a handler at the embassy, just in case of protocol breaches. I'm sure you've got a lot of work ahead, reviewing James's records from the last two visits." He flashes me a lightning grin. "You might as well take a week's leave for sightseeing while you're out there, once the job's done. You can tell me how accurate the book is when you get home."

►◄►◄►◄

Hello. My name is Bob Howard, and I do secret work for the government. Magic is a branch of applied computation, and ever since the invention of the digital computer coincided with the population bubble, the practice of magic has been getting easier. (Brains are computing devices, too, but you really don't want to perform spells with your grey matter—not if you're attached to it.) A big part of the agency's job (we call it the Laundry, because it was headquartered above a Chinese laundry in Soho during the Second World War) is suppressing magical incursions of the "too many tentacles, not enough sanity" variety. And we're losing the fight.

Currently I'm trying to fill the boots of my former superior. Dr. James Angleton (not his real name—true names have power) got himself killed a little over a year ago. He was a heavy hitter, due to not being entirely human: long ago he was turned into the mortal vessel of an ancient power called the Eater of Souls.

A couple of years ago, a bunch of maniacs who had stolen the recipe for summoning the Eater of Souls and binding it to service tried to install it on *my* wetware. The resulting mess left me spiritually entangled with my boss—a kind of deputy assistant understudy Eater of Souls—and now that Dr. Angleton isn't around anymore, I'm the nearest thing the department has to a replacement. They're not happy. Government bureaucracies rely on their public servants being functionally interchangeable, able to pick up one another's briefs and wash away the stains left by their predecessors without any fuss. But my powers aren't readily transferable, so I'm stuck with the job for the foreseeable future, and I'm not happy either.

Angleton's main task was securing the wards locking down contaminated thaumaturgic waste sites—bloodstained eldritch temples, tombs of minor arcane horrors, music festival venues popular with the Azathoth pipe band set. Being ageless, he'd been at it since the 1930s. There are a *lot* of sites, and they need checking regularly. During the Allied occupation of Germany and Japan, Angleton was in much demand—you would not *believe* how many ghastly necromantic relics the Nazis left behind. Not to mention how many Shinto shrines up and down the spine of Honshu are haunted by the hungry ghosts of executed war criminals they still honor (very much a self-inflicted problem, that). I have an uneasy feeling he was mostly there to *monitor* them, rather than help: but it's not as if I can ask him, is it?

And that brings me up to the present: spring, 2014.

According to Angleton's *very brief* notes, most of

the Japanese wartime sites are either dormant or actually certified extinct. But Angleton's full workplace diaries aren't online, either on our intranet or saved as microfiches in his office. When I checked his filing cabinets I found only a dog-eared index card saying he'd sent them down to Archives to save space. And when I dropped in to ask for them, it turned out they'd been misfiled. The Librarian is very helpful and promises to email me a scan as soon as possible—they're old enough that their confidentiality level has decayed from TOP SECRET EYES ONLY to POLITICALLY INCORRECT/QUAINT CURIOSITY, so emailing them is permissible—but in the meantime I'm flying blind.

Which makes the question of why the Miyamoto Group is asking for the Eater of Souls a bit of a head-scratcher. Especially as they want Dr. Angleton to take a look at a site in Tama New Town—which didn't even exist until the 1960s!

I have no idea what's going on but I intend to find out, just as soon as I get over the boss-level jet lag and meet my liaison officer.

► ◄ ► ◄ ◄

The flight from Heathrow to Tokyo is grim. Luckily I've racked up enough air miles in the past year to treat myself to an upgrade, but the time difference gets me all the same. I collect my bag, stumble through an immigration queue and customs, catch a train to Shinjuku, and emerge blinking into midmorning sunlight at what my body insists is 3:00 a.m. Long day ahead.

I have a smartphone. In fact, being sane and traveling on business, I have two. (One's my personal phone, the other is a work-issued device. Guess which has the international roaming data plan?) There's plenty of bandwidth, so I rely on the Google monster to get me out of the nightmarish maze that is Shinjuku station and onto the sidewalk. Ten minutes later—I get lost a couple of times en route, there's a lot of GPS signal bounce due to the skyscrapers, and my app hates the underpasses and pedestrian skywalks—I find myself in the glass-and-marble lobby of the Keio Plaza Hotel, where my hosts have booked me a room.

The immaculately uniformed woman at the front desk gives me a worried smile when I hand her my passport. It takes her a while to find me in the reservations database under Capital Laundry Services, our usual open travel cover. "Ah, sir is entitled to use the Premier counter! Please, follow me?" I'm walked across an expanse of marble to another counter, this time with gold leaf trim, and a most peculiar feeling spills over me, as if I'm very politely being singled out to be the target of an elaborate joke. She passes me over to a fellow in a dark suit so stiffly formal that I wonder if I'm being introduced to my undertaker, and there is some bowing and scraping that my fatigued brain is too dizzy to take in. "Your room key, sir," says the new clerk. "Please follow me?" It is made clear that my suitcase is the responsibility of the porter— white gloves, who the hell wears white gloves to load a baggage cart?—and we waltz off towards an express elevator in one roped-off corner of the lobby.

My room key is pink. And that's all the warning I get before I am led along a hotel corridor that is also pink, to a door with a pink plastic bow above the peep-hole. "Welcome to the Princess Kitty Room!" says my escort. "We hope you enjoy your stay." And he opens the door and bows silently, while I'm still flapping my mouth like a stunned koi.

I wordlessly enter the Princess Kitty Room, where the decor is camp going on kitsch: pink roses on cream wallpaper, mauve rose patterns on pink carpet, magenta bedding and frills and bows and furbelows on *everything*. Despite which, it is still just a room in an

upmarket hotel in the middle of Tokyo, priced somewhere in the stratosphere—I am *really glad* that my
hosts are paying for it, I would *hate* to have to explain
this to the Auditors—and I turn around to thank the
clerk just in time to see the door closing with an almost audible *pop* of soundproofing.

The instant I'm alone, my brain goes into power-
saving mode. I try to fight it off, but I'm totally
jet-lagged and the soporific pink noise of the air-
conditioning is tickling my snore gland. So it takes me
a couple of minutes of fumbling around, unpacking
clothes and plugging in my tangle of low-voltage wall-
warts, before I realize there's a laptop sitting on the
dressing table, waiting for me.

It's a Sony Vaio laptop, with a mauve-and-pink two-
tone shell, and it's open and running a video chat ses-
sion.

Ah.

Under normal circumstances I would think twice
before prodding somebody else's computer. But I'm
guessing this is here for a purpose, so I sit down. Right
now it shows a frozen view of a cramped, windowless
office. But just as I'm asking myself "what happens if I
tweak *this* setting" the windowless office does a really
weird rotate-and-dissolve and is replaced by the face

of a young-ish Japanese woman in office-lady suit, her makeup so immaculate that it looks photoshopped. "Welcome, Dr. Angleton? I am happy to meet you!" she says, and twitches a pointed ear. She has a faint East Coast American accent. She drops her gaze, and I rack my brain for the correct etiquette for this situation. Both of us are outside our comfort zones: she was expecting Angleton, and I was expecting a human being. (Or at least someone more human than I am, these days.)

The ward I wear on a cord round my neck is definitely warm. Suspicion confirmed: the cat ears are real, although she probably wears a concealing glamour in public. They come to delicate tufted points, like a lynx's. They're set forward and high on the cranial dome; if she has regular human ears as well, they're concealed beneath her glossy black hair.

"I'm pleased to meet you too," I say, trying for noncommittal, "but I regret that there seems to be a miscommunication: I'm not Dr. Angleton."

Her smile becomes just slightly rigid. "Oh, I'm so sorry! I am Yoko Suzuki, and I was expecting to welcome Dr. Angleton back to Japan on behalf of the Miyamoto Group. May I ask your name?"

"I'm Bob Howard. I'm afraid Dr. Angleton is

unavailable. I'm his replacement." I stifle a jaw-cracking yawn. "He . . . well, I'm afraid his records of his previous visits here are incomplete, so anything you can tell me would be very helpful. I—" My battle against yawning fails. "Oh, I'm sorry. Long flight!"

Ms. Suzuki, whose expression has gone from one of respectful welcome to implying that I shot her kitten, blinks at me. "Ah, I see." Her gaze slithers sideways, then she inclines her head. "Perhaps we should continue in the morning, in person? You should recover from your journey."

I manage to hold back another cavernous yawn. "Absolutely."

"May I ask when Dr. Angleton will be back at work? I hope all is well with him? I need to inform my superiors. . . ."

I steel myself. "Dr. Angleton was killed in the line of duty last year. He was my boss for seven years before that, so I should be able to duplicate his work." *I hope.* "I inherited his abilities. Should I come to your offices tomorrow, or would you prefer to meet me here?"

She smiles with lips clenched tight, not revealing her fangs. Nevertheless I see a flash of steel behind the mask, quickly hidden: "I'll meet you in the hotel lobby. Shall we say nine o'clock?"

It's a date.

▶▶◀◀

I'm Bob Howard, I do secret work for the government, and I wouldn't normally be seen dead in a suit and tie. But Dr. Armstrong hinted strongly that I should suspend my normal office-casual policy while representing the agency to our Japanese opposite numbers, so I packed my funerals-and-courtroom-appearances suit, which normally lives at the back of the closet except when it's needed for *Men in Black* cosplay parties. It still smells faintly of mothballs as I hang it in the hotel wardrobe. Then I set myself a four-hour timer and climb into the lilac-and-crimson bed for a jet-lag catch-up nap.

The next morning I am just about awake enough to think of all the questions I was too drunk on fatigue poisons to ask yesterday. Such as: Why am I in a luxury hotel room—booked via the Miyamoto Group's liaison people—themed for a cartoon cat? Why wasn't Ms. Suzuki told to expect me, instead of James? Why, for that matter, does my assigned interpreter have nekomimi ears? But first: *breakfast*.

I find my way back to the elevator, noting with approval that there aren't any unmarked staff-only doors on my short route: portals into hotelspace are always bad news. Yes, you can sometimes find a shortcut from your Ibis Styles bedroom into your hotel's dining room via a Kimpton laundry, but you're equally likely to end up in a boarded-up railway hotel in Middlesbrough. So I avoid the ghost roads and stay within the bounds of architecture as I go in search of food.

There is a very neat and tidy hotel restaurant with a breakfast buffet. Three different breakfast buffets, in fact: a Japanese one, an Indian one, and a Western one. Which looks like absolutely no cooked English breakfast I've ever seen, but I give the scrambled egg and bacon-adjacent product baked into a Yorkshire pudding a chance to settle my stomach before I drown it in filter coffee.

Once fortified I head back to my room. I shower, shave, and dress in the monkey suit, it having been impressed upon me that Japanese workplace expectations are weirdly mired in the 1950s, then head down to the lobby.

I'm a couple of minutes early, but Ms. Suzuki is waiting for me, along with a skinny bloke with glasses and a small goatee which marks him out as a dangerous eccentric. They're both wearing funereal black suits, more formal than bank managers back home. I try to remember what I was told about how and when to bow, but give up when Ms. Suzuki smiles and Mr. Goatee grabs my hand and pumps it vigorously, American style. She introduces him: "This is Dr. Hasakawa, from the Department of Apocryphal Organisms," she explains.

"I am very pleased to meet you," he says painfully.

"Likewise," I say, and he looks blank. I've clearly overrun his high-school English, and Ms. Suzuki cuts in cleanly, with some sort of long-winded introduction. While she's speaking I realize that I'm seeing things, or rather not seeing things: were the cat ears last night just a headband thing after all? Because they're not in evidence today.

"I will interpret," she says, "and introduce? Yes. Dr. Hasakawa is a specialist in the study and suppression of yokai infestations, such as the sites Dr. Angleton assisted us with previously." I notice that her voice rises about an octave, into a higher register, when she addresses Mister—no, Doctor—Goatee in Japanese. "A car is waiting to take you to the first site! It is some distance away, so there is time to brief you en route."

Before I quite figure out what's going on I find myself in the back seat of an anonymous silver Toyota—all the cars here seem to be silver or white, except for a sprinkling of boxy taxis that look like they've fallen out of a sixties movie—across an armrest from Ms. Suzuki. Dr. Hasakawa is in the passenger seat up front, beside a driver who is wearing a peak-brimmed cap and white gloves, because obviously that's the uniform chauffeurs wear. There are even lace doilies on the seat headrests.

Ms. Suzuki pulls out a yellowing sheaf of typed notes and presents them to me. "We have a busy itinerary this morning, but the director has requested the pleasure of your company for lunch—there is an excellent restaurant near our headquarters—and I thought you would like to review the notes for the secondary sites this afternoon before we begin work tomorrow. If you give me your nonsecure phone, I will add our contacts to it. Is that all right?" she adds, almost as an afterthought. I glance at the back of Doc Goatee's head, then see from the rearview mirror that his eyes are closed and he's snoring softly, like a puppet that's been put down between acts.

"I'll deal," I say. Then, as we pull out into the dense stop-and-go traffic I add quietly, "What's *really* going on here?"

Ms. Suzuki gives me an opaque look: "I don't know what you mean," she says, but one hand nervously smooths her skirt over her knees. "Is something wrong with the hotel?"

"Nothing is wrong with the hotel." Nothing except that the decor in my room's so sugary it sets my teeth on edge. "But delivering a briefing in a car, really? Are there no secure meeting rooms in your headquarters? Also"—I nod at the front passenger seat—"your beard is askew, Ms. Suzuki. Or should that be Dr. Suzuki?"

"Oh dear, he dozes off at the *most* inconvenient times." She glares at Dr. Hasakawa, in a manner that makes it clear that all the western stereotypes about Japanese people being hard to read are as wide of the mark as sexist stereotypes about Japanese women. Yoko Suzuki is clearly pissed-off and working to control it. "Why don't you tell me what *you* think is going on, Mr. Howard?" She makes a subtle gesture with her right hand and my ears pop. The windows dim and all sound beyond the bench seat we share is muted, even as our driver turns onto a slip road and grinds to a halt as he attempts to merge with a crowded stretch of urban motorway.

I think for a moment. "The Miyamoto Group is legendarily competent," I begin, then stop.

Every Great Power established an occult operations agency between the world wars, but not all of them survived intact. Established—or rather, *re-*established—during the American occupation after the Second World War, the Miyamoto Group was initially monitored closely and required to model their institutional practices on their American counterparts. (Their 1931–45 predecessors were not considered to be a suitable role model, to say the least.)

"Back in the late forties my predecessors and the OPA"—the Operational Phenomenology Agency, the American occult agency also known as the Black Chamber (never call them the Nazgül where they might overhear you)—"worked together more closely than is now the case." (Which is a massive understatement, but that's another story.) "Even so, I can't imagine anyone from the OPA or the Miyamoto Group was keen to request the assistance of the Eater of Souls. Or to *be seen* requesting it."

"It's bad for one's promotion prospects," she agrees.

"Looks weak, doesn't help justify increased budget requests." I suddenly wonder just how much Angleton—or his understudy, that being me—is billed at per hour to sister agencies.

"Where did you study?" I ask.

"Computer Science at MIT, then Arkham, for my master's. Tokyo for my PhD. Why? What gave me away?"

I very deliberately glance at the front seat. "Eh. Your English is perfect, but your interpreter act was a bit less polished. I've been traveling a lot this year and simultaneous translation is—well, you get to recognize the cadence. Why the beard?"

"He's not *just* an assistant, he really *does* have a doctorate in alarmingly relevant folklore. But requesting the assistance of an English demon like the Eater of Souls isn't the only thing that's bad for one's promotion prospects in my organization, Mr. Howard. Being female is another, and being born *yokai* is a third." She nods at the puppet: "Ren will be fine: he just has asynchronous narcolepsy. I brought him along because it's easier if he does the talking in certain situations."

"So right now the job involves cleaning up something smelly that my predecessor left behind, and which needs to be kept at arm's reach from the organization lest the smell annoy those with more sensitive nostrils?" I suspect the closest I'm going to get to HQ is doing lunch with a middle manager in a restaurant around the corner—assuming he's not just another of Dr. Suzuki's Bunraku puppets. A second thought strikes me. "Am I right in thinking Dr. Angleton didn't make a good impression last time he was here?"

She smiles at me as if I'm a slow primary kid who has just mastered his first syllabary: "Correct, Mr. Howard! You were our third choice—regrettably, Beijing and Seoul both declined to help. But let me set your mind at ease: this is an excellent opportunity for you to redeem my superiors' opinion of your organization. First, please familiarize yourself with the synopsis of the first site on our itinerary this morning. We will arrive in less than an hour and you need to be prepared."

►◄►◄►◄

Let's be clear about one thing: Dr. Yoko Suzuki is softening me up. Easing me in. Lulling me into a false sense of security. I've been on the receiving end of this treatment before. She's also really pissed about something, is only partially successful in bottling it up, and some of the leakage is spraying in my direction. Let's see: Can we guess what it is?

My illustrious predecessor was asked to do a job the Miyamoto Group wasn't up to—worse, he was asked to come back to rebind it *twice*, meaning it was a tough one, and even after watching him work they couldn't figure out how to duplicate his efforts themselves. That's strike one. It'd be as serious a loss of face in London as it is here in Japan. (Bringing in outside help is a tacit admission of institutional incompetence.) Strike two . . . let me guess: Angleton was old—he formed his social attitudes in the early years of the twentieth century and first visited Japan during the postwar occupation, primed by years of racist propaganda. Nobody would accuse him of being an enlightened and sensitive soul at the best of times, and I'm guessing he stomped hard on the sensibilities of some people who are now *quite* senior. Worst of all: whatever he did was something to do with the Department of Apocryphal Organisms, which means it has landed in Dr. Suzuki's lap, so my presence here is an implicit slight to her competence. *Great.*

The Foreign Office provides helpful cultural background briefings for those of us representing our agencies abroad, and I read mine on the flight over.

According to the FO, Dr. Yoko Suzuki exists in a work-place environment that is roughly as sexist and racist as the UK was in the mid-1960s. Women are second-class citizens, as are foreigners. Fetching and carrying the coffee? Check. Mandatory heels and makeup? Check. Fired if she gets married or falls pregnant? Check. Passed over for promotion every time in favor of lucky idiots who just happen to possess a Y-chromosome or the right pedigree? Check. Yet despite all the shit, here she is with a PhD and a key position, not to mention a male sock puppet for deflecting sexist idiots who mistake her for a secretary. Which all means that she's a terrifyingly efficient overachiever, and consequently gets the crap. She gritted her teeth and put in a request for assistance from the offensive foreign force of super-nature that had done the job twice before . . . only to get *me*. Unknown, untried, and not exactly terrifying—unlike Angleton.

No wonder she's pissed.

I'm still a bit jet-laggy so the first job of the morning goes by in a blur. Dr. Hasakawa wakes up in time to lead us under a red-and-gold-painted gate with an arched roof. It's set between a crowded shopping mall and an electronics store. We file along a stone-flagged path that leads to a square that is almost completely filled by a Buddhist temple about as old as the Tower of London. It's charming, eccentric, and there are monks in saffron robes with iPhones playing J-pop ringtones. Dr. Hasakawa bows, then engages in a brief pleased-to-meet-you-someone-called-us-to-fix-the-plumbing with a bald guy who appears from his pained smile to be absolutely desperate to get the toilet flushing again. I am introduced: there is more bowing. Yoko stands behind us with hands clasped, staring at her shoes. Evidently she's expected to pretend to be part of the furniture.

The temple is an airy structure of polished wooden floors and movable rice-paper screens held in wooden frames. We are led through a series of corridors to a room at the back of the temple. It appears to be some sort of store closet, going by the mops and buckets and the suspicious stains on the floor, and it's deep enough inside that illumination comes from a single bare-filament light bulb that glimmers as if it's on the brink of burnout. The wall screens are grubby and ne-glected, and as I approach the back of the room my ward begins to buzz like an angry wasp.

Yoko, her face fixed, makes a good fist of interpret-ing: "This is the site of the first haunting we need to deal with today. It's a moderately powerful Mokumoku

Ren"—she gestures at one of the sliding lattice screens—
"and it moved in last week. I would—*Dr. Hasakawa*
would—like you to get rid of it, if you please. Just move
it on?" She turns back to Dr. Hasakawa and Brother
Abbot, smiles and bobs, and explains something to
them in Japanese. Once again I bitterly regret my lack
of language skills: she might as well be saying *we are
sorry to keep you waiting, all our agents are currently
engaged, your call is valuable to us* for all I can tell.

"A Mokumoku Ren is what, exactly?" I ask.

She rolls her eyes when her back is turned to the
Brother Abbot. "See for yourself."

I open my inner eye and look at the screen and it
looks back at me, and I have to admit: I'm the one who
blinks first.

"You have *got* to be shitting me."

I don't realize I've spoken aloud until Yoko clears
her throat: "Excuse me?" Then I look round and see
that Dr. Hasakawa and Brother Abbot are watching
me expectantly.

"Can they see it?" I ask: "Can *you*?"

She nods. "Describe it, please." For a moment I can
see her standing confidently in front of a lecture hall
full of American students, holding forth with authority.

"It's . . ." I sigh. "The walls have eyes." Lots and

lots of eyes. Most of them closed and sleeping right now, just holes in the moth-eaten paper panels, but—"What happens when they wake up?"

"Not much. They scare people, but they're not actively dangerous most of the time. Legends of them stealing unwary sleepers' eyeballs cannot be confirmed in the laboratory. Can you banish it?"

I side-eye her. This isn't anything they'd need to call in Angleton to deal with. It's trivial. *So, a test.* "Do you have any constraints on my methods?" I ask. Like, *do not detonate happy fun temple while banishing minor irritant.* Behind her, Doc Sleepy engages Brother Abbot in animated conversation about . . . something. (I hate not being able to understand the people around me.)

"Please do not use any computational assistance? I would like to see the scope of your own power," she says.

Well, that's me told. I leave my phone in my jacket pocket and stare at the haunted screen door. "*You,*" I snap, in English: "*piss off.*" And I put just enough of my will behind my words to drive the point home.

The Mokumoku Ren is basically just your run-of-the-mill extradimensional eater—and a rather pathetic specimen at that: a parasitic pattern that latches onto neural networks and feeds on the entropy they generate as they mutate input images. If I had a copy of the classic Deep Dreams GAN running on my phone I could hypnotize (or feed) the hell out of this thing, but I'm in no mood to waste time, so what I do is about as subtle as punching my fist through its abdomen and pulling its still-beating heart out through its ribs. If it had an abdomen, heart, and rib cage, of course.

The response is near-instant: a deafening psychic screech like tearing metal, a stink of ozone, a horrible splattery sensation as if I just rammed my fingertips into a bucket of raw eyeballs (this last may be psychosomatic because that's pretty much exactly what I just did)—and the Mokumoku Ren explodes. The light bulb pops, leaving us in total darkness. Doc Sleepy shouts, and Brother Abbot rapidly tells him something; then, a moment later, Dr. Suzuki switches on a penlight. Clasped in front of her, it casts deep shadows that lend her face a spectral, almost satanic aspect as she smiles and bows and explains something to Brother Abbot. Who slides another panel open, and we exit the store closet through the back of the dining room.

"Did he perform satisfactorily?" I hear Doc Sleepy ask Yoko in Old Enochian, which just happens to be a language I *do* speak.

"*He appears to be adequate, although his form is lamentable*," she tells her colleague, then switches to English to address me: "Quickly! There's no time to waste! The companion infestation is just around the corner. This type of incursion always manifests in pairs." And she leads me right across the road to a kitchenware store where something special is lurking behind the Crock-Pots.

I carefully show no sign of understanding their brief conversation about me as we leave the temple grounds—if I was a monoglot anglophone with no understanding of the tongue of ritual magic I might have missed it completely—but inwardly I'm quietly seething. I'm determined to show them: I'm just not sure what, yet.

▶◀▶◀▶

By the end of the first day I am well and truly done with this *Ghostbusters/Men in Black* LARP. But as a Japanese Navy officer (allegedly) said in 1944, the beatings will continue until morale improves.

After zapping the eyes without a face—twice—Yoko drags me into a hotel (subtype: downmarket business travelers, not rich Chinese tourists) where I get to walk face-first into a Nurikabe in the fourth-floor laundry room. The Nurikabe is an invisible, intangible obstacle, an immaterial roadblock: suffice to say, it doesn't last long. The fact that there's a second one in the basement is just plain annoying, but there *is* a hotelspace shortcut, and I think I startle Yoko slightly when I make use of it to sneak up on the low-rent gelatinous cube. Next, she takes me to a boys' secondary school where a Namahage is hibernating behind the HVAC installation. The sight of a scary fanged haystack snoring with its hands around the handle of a machete does not fill me with good vibes, but it looks a whole lot more materially real than the first two: I lead my escorts back around the side of the building before I ask, "Do you want it dead? Because I don't think this one is just going to go away if I tell it to leave."

Dr. Suzuki gives me an even stare. "Whatever it takes," she says, with great deliberation.

"Okay, but someone else is disposing of the remains."

"*Whatever it takes*," she repeats firmly. She's holding a clipboard and a pen, and judging from her expression I'm not supposed to be asking questions in the middle of an exam.

I walk back around the side of the building. The

Namahage is snoring softly to itself, presumably dreaming of chillblains and idlers. I'm not sure what it did to the Miyamoto Group to deserve them dropping the Eater of Souls on it, but I steel myself and open my mouth—not the one my dentist is on professional terms with, but the imaginary one that haunts my nightmares—and without giving it the slightest warning, I go *chomp*.

Let me tell you: Namahage soul tastes *disgusting*. Especially when I then have to repeat the banishment with its twin bunion troll in the stationery closet. What is it with these things and their affinity for service spaces that abut the paths behind the world?

I really don't like this bad-things-come-in-twos shtick. There's something hinky about it.

At lunchtime Dr. Suzuki takes me to a French restaurant back in the center—in Shibuya, I think; my Tokyo geography is woefully vague. She introduces me to a painfully polite managerial dude in an expensive suit, then leaves us. Dude-in-a-suit, whose English is only marginally better than my Japanese, escorts me to a table at one end of the dining room. Here I am introduced to Mr. Hiroshi, a sprightly seventy-something with silver hair and a *very* expensively tailored suit, who casually mentions that his family owns the restaurant. It is somehow implied that he's strato-spherically senior within the Miyamoto Group. Mr. Hiroshi speaks perfect English with an accent that would be perfectly at home in the Oxford Union—he studied in the UK in the seventies, apparently. "Do, please, accept my deepest sympathies for James, as well as my congratulations on your promotion." I do not fail to notice the ambiguity. "And please pass on my condolences to Michael. I assume he's still in Audit? It's been such a long time since I was stationed in London . . ."

I am on my best behavior and therefore pay barely any attention to the Michelin-starred meal because I'm desperately trying not to screw up and inadvertently offend my hosts. The vibe I got from Dr. Suzuki is strong here: Angleton did *not* endear himself to my hosts, and they're doing me a special favor by giving me this once-in-a-working-lifetime opportunity to prove that not *all* British operatives are assholes. Mr. Hiroshi's skin has a peculiar liminal glow that hints at otherworldly connections. I've met his ilk before in the offices on Mahogany Row, gliding like great predatory sharks beneath the still waters of organizational politics. Offending him would be *bad*. As I contemplate a glass of ridiculously smooth single malt, Mr.

Hiroshi turns to business. He smiles at me, then asks, "And how has your morning been so far?"

"It's—" I have to kick-start my work-brain. "—it's been rather educational. I didn't realize there was such a problem with yokai taking up residence in the Greater Tokyo area. Or that they always come in pairs—that's not something we get back at home." For which I'm very grateful: exorcising just the one haunted English Electric Lightning interceptor was more than enough, thank you very much. "Is it a long-standing problem?"

"Mm, you could say that." He pauses to sip his whisky. "They've always been around, but got somewhat scarce after the Meiji Restoration. Then they gradually became a problem again over the last sixty years. They correlate strongly with population density and computational activity—Akihabara was a particular hot spot until about five years ago, you know. It's the elevated thaum flux we're experiencing. When the background level of mana is high enough, we can see spontaneous yokai-antiyokai pair production—like high energy photons that produce virtual positron-electron pairs. If they meet they mutually annihilate, but chasing down a pair of monsters and banging them together inside a containment grid is significantly harder than dealing with them piecemeal. You should stick close to Dr. Suzuki and listen to her advice: she's extremely competent." There is a slight emphasis on the word *should*. "However, yokai aren't our biggest problem."

"Oh?"

"The Kaiju threat level is higher than it's been for *centuries*." He puts his glass down heavily. "They do not closely match their movie representations, Gojira and Mothra and I don't know what. But they're based on legends of, ah, I suppose you would say mega-yokai? Gashadokoru—giant skeletal bone monsters spawned by wars and famines—stuff like that. A regular yokai infestation is bad enough, but if the thaum flux rises significantly higher"—which is happening worldwide; the Laundry even has a codename for this, CASE NIGHTMARE GREEN, the magical equivalent of anthropogenic climate change—"we run the risk of catastrophic reification, whereby the thaum field undergoes a phase-state transition, collapsing from a distributed yokai probability cloud into a single monolithic intrusion. Instead of a swarm of pests, we would then face a giant existential threat. Thankfully we don't have many rifts—*hellmouths,* I think, is the colloquialism: James assisted in locking down the worst of them, in his own abrasive way. But the one in Tama is giving us cause for concern." He makes eye contact, and suddenly I get *exactly* the same bug-on-a-microscope-slide sensation that Angleton could induce with a glance: a queasy icy tickle on the back of my neck that says *this is what you're here for, this is the real deal.* And it's not the Mickey Mouse corner-shop hauntings Dr. Suzuki and Super Snore Boy have been dragging me round all morning: it's a goddamn hellmouth that needs sealing.

"In all seriousness, if you doubt your competence to deputize for the Eater of Souls, it would be better to say so than to press ahead blindly. You can rely on my silence if you need to withdraw discreetly. James was very much one of a kind, and there is no shame in the journeyman admitting that he is not yet the master."

I throw my napkin on the table. "It would have helped if I'd been fully informed about the Tama site before I came here," I tell him bluntly. "Dr. Angleton's records were disorganized at the time of his death." (Which isn't surprising, if he made as much of a pig's ear of the liaison side of the mission as I'm coming to suspect.) I lean forward. "As it happens, I *have* inherited his power"—his connection to the ancient hungry ghost known as the Eater of Souls—"although I lack his depth of experience." When he died, Angleton was over a century old, although he looked like a well-preserved sixty-something: being the living avatar of an ancient evil is surprisingly good for the skin. "My biggest problem is not any lack of power, but a lack of context. My briefing at home was clearly inadequate, and I would appreciate whatever up-to-date information you can provide. Going in without adequate preparation isn't good for anyone. Is there a file on Tama?"

"Mm-hmm, yes, but it's written in Japanese, for which I make no apologies." He shows me a brief grimace of faux-embarrassment. "Dr. Suzuki will give you a synopsis, then she can accompany you when you tour the site. Probably the day after tomorrow at this point, it's getting late. Well, I should let you get back to your familiarization tour with Yoko, I believe she's eager to show you some of our more obstreperous neighbors before it's time to meet the big one! Just to get you used to handling yokai."

I have been performing banishments and field exorcisms for most of a decade at this point, but there's nothing to be gained by pointing this out, so I just smile politely and nod. The maître d' comes and helps Mr. Hiroshi out of his chair. Then Yoko, who appears to have been waiting in the wings the whole time (unless she sneaked off to a salad bar while Mr. Hiroshi was pinning my ears back), comes to take me away.

"Did you enjoy your lunch?" she asks me as she steers me back towards the car park.

"It was—" I don't actually remember it. "—rather good," I temporize. "But I don't enjoy being given the runaround. If you asked for me because of Tama, why not cut to the chase? Why all the crap little jobs?"

"Because Tama is different." Dr. Suzuki side-eyes me skeptically. "The 'little jobs,' as you call them, give us a degree of confidence in your abilities. We've had bad experiences with foreign liaison officers in the past. They come in, make wild promises, then leave a mess behind."

I nod. "Angleton," I say blandly. "Or was it his manners?"

"I wasn't here, I really couldn't say."

"He could be rather abrasive," I concede. Abrasive like diamond-grit paper.

"Perhaps. But I am more concerned about Tama. The manifestation there is simply too big to take any risks with. We are supposed to visit four more sites today, and then we can return you to your hotel. Tomorrow—" Her phone trills, and she glances at it. "I'll take you to Tama for a site visit. It's a little irregular, but it might be best to get you oriented as soon as possible. The day after, we can start planning how to lock it down. I expect it will take at least a week." We come to the car park entrance where our driver is waiting. He bows to Dr. Suzuki, then feeds a smartcard into a slot by a garage door. There is much clanking and whirring, and then the door opens like the world's largest vending machine and disgorges a silver Toyota. It may or may not be the same one as this morning's ride. We get in, and he whisks us off to the haunted library or animated lantern or tofu monster or whatever the hell they want to score me on next.

►◄►◄►◄

I have to settle the accounts of four more paired reifications of batshit Japanese folklore before Drs. Suzuki and Hasakawa agree to call it a day. Along the way I learn that while the yokai are powered by the magic pollution emitted by all the computing appliances in Greater Tokyo, they're given shape by the beliefs and hopes and fears of the general public. They tend to crop up in couples near sites where the walls between the worlds are thin—service tunnels, temples, university supercomputing centers. I should count myself lucky that Japan gets dragon ladies and Tsukumo-gami rather than zombies and human sacrifice cults. The yokai and kami of this land, its monsters and spirits, are capricious, sometimes dangerous, but tend to be more in line with traditional expectations. They're also *slightly* less inclined to dementedly bloodthirsty violence than the eldritch denizens of Dewsbury. Even so, I am a jelly-kneed, aching mess when my minders drop me back in the hotel lobby at six o'clock.

I lean drunkenly against the mirrored wall of the elevator, stagger to my room, and leave a trail of clothing all the way to the shower. After ten minutes under a stream of hot water I feel slightly more human, so I engage in single combat with the smart toilet (*why* does a toilet need a graphical user interface and a heated seat? I mean, *really?*), brush my teeth, plug my phones in to recharge, and lie down for a brief nap.

When I awaken two hours later, night has fallen, dimming the sky to a dusky orange glow of street lights reflecting off the clouds overhead. It's nearly nine, which is way too early to go to bed. But lunch has long since receded in the rearview mirror and my stomach is rumbling, so I grab my work phone, pull on a T-shirt and jeans, and head downstairs.

Things I notice about exploring Tokyo in the dark, walking off the tail end of jet lag: at least they drive on the right side of the road—that is, on the left—so I'm looking the correct way when I try to cross at the lights. High-rise buildings tower everywhere, densely packed but without the grim canyonlike intensity of Manhattan. The unreadable illuminated signs give me a weird throwback feeling, as if I'm three years old and preliterate all over again. Shops play loud music through speakers over open doorways, blasting out air-conditioning set to stun—not that it's needed: it's pleasantly warm, but the full heat of summer hasn't arrived yet. When I pull up Google Maps and ask about food it directs me to a department store. According to the English-language store guide, the seventh floor is a food court. I ride the escalators all the way up and find myself in a mazelike warren packed with tiny restaurants, half of them closed. Plastic models of the dishes they offer occupy window displays, gleaming like waxworks beneath paper lanterns. Then a series of musical chimes and a multilingual announcement informs me that the department store is closing. So much for supper.

Eventually I find a hole-in-the-wall noodle bar in a side street, where tired-looking locals nurse chipped ceramic bowls of ramen. I order by pointing at a picture and handing over a banknote, and presently find myself slurping from a steaming bowl of soup.

As I head back to my hotel I notice that I am being followed by a giant pink-and-white anthropomorphic cat wearing a dress with more flounces than a 1990s usenet flame war. She's handing out flyers. When she mimes for my attention I take one, shove it in my pocket, and say, "Thank you." She curtseys in gratitude (I suspect because if she tried to bow her giant bobble-head would cause her to topple over). As I walk away I glance across the street and see a black-and-white cat with a perspex helmet, evidently an astro-cat, be-having similarly. Beyond the next crossroads an angry penguin is canvassing for . . . what? This is unknow-able, especially in my current headspace, for right now the velvet hammer of jet lag is coming down hard on my consciousness, and if challenged to chew gum as I walk I'd probably trip over my own feet.

I pick up my personal phone and my thumb hov-ers over my Favorites contact list. I want to hear Mo's voice, but I'm so tired I'm afraid of accidentally an-noying her. Also, it's still core working hours back in Blighty. Knowing my luck she'll probably be in a meet-ing. I waver for a moment, then put the phone down.

Calling will have to wait until I'm sufficiently acclimatized to make sense at one in the morning. Instead, I update my notes, logging every site I visited today while I can still remember them.

The last thing I remember before I crawl into bed is plugging my phones back in and chucking the pamphlet on top of the mauve-and-pink laptop my hosts left me. Then I'm out like a light—until the dreams begin.

▶◀▶◀▶◀

I am dreaming, and in my dream I am in church, naked from the waist down. But that's okay, because so is the rest of the congregation.

The weird bit is not the unscheduled underpants deficiency but the being in church. I don't do churches. I grew up in a nonobservant household, raised atheist by default until I lost my disbelief. Now that I know the gods are real, I would never willingly engage in any act of worship—it only encourages the bastards.

The church is a modern building, light and airy, with bleached pine and tall windows. The walls are draped with pink satin banners. So far, so church. But then the details begin to sink in. While the layout is regular church-modernist, the symbol on the wall behind the pulpit is a big capital *R* unevenly superimposed over a circle. *Isn't that the Happy Science logo?* I wonder. But then I spot Princess Kitty officiating behind the altar, and when I see her mouthless face I realize that this isn't a human being in a wired-and-padded fabric kitty suit; this is the actual living, breathing incarnation of the Kami of Kitsch. She sits atop a backless stool in lotus pose, much like a statue of the Buddha, if Buddha was a cartoon cat in a giant frothy wedding cake gown. She has no mouth but she can sing: Kitty is leading the service, but as she's trilling in Japanese I'm completely at sea.

As church services go—I'm no expert—there seems to be an alarmingly cheerful vibe, not to mention mandatory audience participation. I've really got to hand it to my subconscious: if it weren't for the lack of pants and Pastor Pussycat, I could almost believe it was real. Catchy J-pop music plays through hidden speakers, and Kitty periodically breaks into song, then leads a call and response that everyone in the congregation is familiar with except for me. There is bopping and swaying and dancing in the pews. There is much finger-clicking. Then the music pauses, and Kitty declaims a squeaky visionary sermon with much gesticulation.

Her claws flex and retract when she spreads her arms in benediction, just like a real feline's. A chorus line of bare-arsed cultists prance onto the raised podium behind Princess Kitty and begin a vigorous dance aerobics routine. Then Kitty makes some kind of significant announcement. Her voice, thin and piping, reminds me somehow of a monstrous unseen flute. She strikes a pose behind the pulpit as a squad of enthusiastic worshippers drag a bound and writhing Dr. Suzuki to the altar, apparently to provide a real blood-and-flesh sacrifice for their bizarre eucharist.

At this point I dream that the dream is turning bad, so I dream that I make a determined effort to wake up—or at least to rise into a lucid state, in hope that I can then hit the "off" switch. (I've had lucid dreams before, and in my experience they're the fastest route out of a nightmare.) It may be just a night terror, but I still don't want to see Princess Kitty disembowel Dr. Suzuki with an obsidian hand-axe that looks to have come straight out of a Mesoamerican temple; and anyway, knowing how my power works, I'm not betting on it staying a dream.

Bizarrely, Yoko is wearing a gothic Lolita frock as overblown as Kitty's. She's putting up a fight despite being gagged, bound, and held down by half a dozen

beaming cultists. Her fingers curl into clawlike mu-
dras, sparks glowing around her nail beds. Her cat
ears are flattened back against her scalp in anger and
she looks furious, eyes promising hell unleashed for
anyone who gets in her way. Then she sees me and
her expression slides into slack-jawed betrayal. That's
all it takes to get me on my feet and moving, pushing
through the congregants as she redoubles her writhing. Suddenly I'm clear of the throng, standing before
Kitty and the altar.

Princess Kitty doesn't speak—she has no mouth—
but she's clearly angry with me for interrupting her
ceremony. And she's taller than I am. She grows by
the second, her shadow lengthening as she looms over
me. The church is darkening, the light reddening to
carmine as her fangs lengthen in jaws that suddenly
gape without a face to frame them. I hear a distant
bell tolling. Dr. Suzuki gets a leg free and kicks one of
the chorus in the balls, rolls off the altar, and scrapes
her duct-taped wrists across their fallen dagger. I only
catch glimpses of her escape because I've got more than
enough trouble of my own: Princess Kitty hisses like a
venting steam locomotive and lunges at me. I duck and
open my inner mouth, the ghost anatomy I acquired
with my elevation to the Eater of Souls, but somehow

I feel oddly congested, my jaws weak and incapable of biting down on her as the bell grows louder—

I open my eyes. It's morning and I'm awake, so why do I feel an unbearable sense of dread? Is my subconscious trying to tell me I've bitten off more than I can chew this time? Fuck knows, but my phone is ringing; time to find out, I guess.

►◄►◄►◄

I'm so disturbed by my nightmare that I forget to shave before my shower. Then I'm late for breakfast, and as I wait for the elevator back to my room (where all the Kitty kitsch has taken on a new and unwelcome significance) I realize I'm even more late. So I barely pause to grab my wallet and phone and head straight back down to the lobby to meet my local handlers. And that's when I realize I've forgotten my necktie.

Dr. Suzuki is waiting for me on her own in the lobby. She's swapped yesterday's office-lady uniform for a grey trouser-suit with low heels and a white shirt buttoned to her chin. I'm not sure what the change signifies: maybe they do casual Friday here and as a special concession she's allowed to wear grey, but she seems so uptight that I wonder (guiltily and inappropriately) if she starches her pajamas. She accessorizes with a black hair band, positioned so that if her cat ears manifest they'll appear to be attached to it. *Nice.* "What's the itinerary for today?" I ask.

"Coffee first!" Yoko offers me a condescending smile. It's a very British smile, tight-lipped rather than an American admire-my-dental-bill gape. It telegraphs the kind of sympathy you offer a colleague who clearly had one too many drinks the night before and doesn't remember what he said. "After that, we can go over today's itinerary."

There is a café off in one side of the hotel lobby. I drink a very expensive latte and we go over a list of lesser manifestations of chaos. There's a pier in Odaiba that has a bad problem with Funa-yurei—ship ghouls, the souls of drowned sailors—scaring the bejesus out of the Korean and Chinese tourists on the sightseeing boats (which is very bad for business at the local shopping mall). A cat café in Shibuya has a Neko-mata tom who sprays everywhere. Apparently, whenever someone tries to trap him and take him to be fixed he goes to ground in the nearest graveyard. Vets and coarse-mannered two-tailed tomcats with a zombie-raising habit, you know the drill. *That* problem I address by suggesting a side-quest to a pet supply shop that sells high-grade catnip. We expense a couple of baggies and a cat carrier, and Yoko wears a surgical mask while I play the part of feline drug pusher. (Felix's twin is not our problem: it was hit and killed by a delivery van a week ago.)

"This is bullshit," I protest after the third site visit. We're scheduled for a lunch break anyway. "I mean, this is some gold-plated intern-grade bullshit. You realize this?"

To her credit, Yoko rolls her eyes. "I know this. You know this. But you must complete the training and evaluation course satisfactorily before my superiors will agree to my asking you to fix the real problem." She shrugs apologetically. "It's the paperwork. And also the precedent set by your predecessor."

Oh for fuck's sake is something I do not say aloud, but think vehemently at my coffee while I count to FF in hexadecimal. Eventually I trust myself enough to take a deep breath and say, "I see."

Dr. Suzuki diplomatically changes the subject. "As you have doubtless realized, these yokai incursions cluster, and it is not a coincidence. We asked for assistance because the clustering has been recorded at least five times in the past—three of them in the last century, before the current outbreak. A hungry ghost works best, but we don't currently have one on payroll and the Korean and Chinese ones are in high demand. We're not the only organization with containment issues at present."

"When I got back to my room last night I logged the ones I've already done on OpenStreetMaps," I admit. "The pattern of clustering is notable. I assume you're ahead of me? Am I right in thinking they don't normally happen this often either?"

"Very good, yes! Normally we would expect two or three per year in the entire Greater Tokyo area. We dealt with twenty-two of them in the six weeks before you arrived, and the list is currently growing by more than one a day, following a Poisson distribution around the epicenter. At the current rate of increase it should become critical sometime in the next week."

"And the epicenter is . . . ?" I prompt as she leads me towards the car waiting outside the lobby. I think I already know the answer, but confirmation is always good.

"It used to be in open countryside, until the 1960s when they built Tama New Town right on top of it. And the . . . I think the term is 'hellmouth' . . . is right under the amusement park. Where we are going after lunch! We can spend the afternoon enjoying the theme park! Don't look so gloomy, it will be fun!"

"That depends on your definition of fun . . ."

► ◄ ► ◄ ►◄

We eat lunch in a small diner in the food court of a department store, where I inhale a bowl of oyaku-don. Dr. Suzuki isn't talkative over food, and after lunch she walks me back to my hotel—"I have to get something: I'll meet you in an hour," she tells me—so I have time to think, alone in my room. I can put two and two together, and for the other stuff I have the Google monster.

The only theme park Tama is famous for is an indoor Disneyworld knock-off called Puroland, run by Sanrio company—the people who created Princess Kitty and friends. They're a corporation with an annual turnover of a quarter of a billion dollars, and their entire shtick is inventing happy shiny anthropomorphic cartoon characters that can be used to shift bucketloads of colorful plastic merchandise aimed at the kawaii market. Which explains my hotel room and the lavender laptop of love (yes, there's a red love-heart on its lid, where a Californian Fruit Corporation machine would have a featureless glowing logo with a missing bite). The Miyamoto Group didn't put me up in the Princess Kitty suite for no reason: they were easing me in tactfully. The dominos are falling. Something's coming through, something otherworldly, something associated with the Mouthless One—She Who Cutes in Pink.

I've got a bad feeling.

While I'm sharing some quality time with my electric shaver, my work phone chimes a ringtone I've assigned for incoming secure business email. I pick it up and swear: someone at the New Annex is working really *odd* hours. At any rate, it's the archival scan I requested, of Angleton's notes from his Japan visits. Which is great, except the munchkins have sent them as a high-resolution PDF, which means it's almost unreadable on my antiquated phone's four-inch screen. (Facilities don't hand out iPhone upgrades whenever Apple holds an event to say "new shiny, cough up!"—so I'm about three generations behind the curve.) I'm about to start reading it on my laptop when my alarm rings. I guess it'll have to wait until this evening.

Yoko is waiting for me in the lobby. Her collar is unbuttoned, displaying a choker with a big opalescent stone dangling from it. Something about it sets my teeth on edge. "What's *that*?" I ask, not even trying to be subtle.

"It's my soul-stone. Are you ready to go?"

"Um—" *Soul-stone* is one hell of a non sequitur. "—after you."

Apparently today we're using public transport. She leads me through the organized chaos of Shinjuku station to a platform signposted by a cartoon rabbit in uniform. We catch a subway train out to the suburbs. I can't read the ads suspended from the ceiling, but going by the happy smiley rainbows and the excited pink speech bubbles rising from the sugarbunnies I suspect they're selling Sanrio baby crack for the terminally hypersquee cuteness addict. (Folks with Type I diabetes: check your blood sugar level *right now*.)

We exit the Tama New Town station into a pedestrianized outdoor mall, where strips of raised yellow bricks lead us past a series of smiling happy cartoon animal sculptures, towards a giant arched rainbow awning. It all seems very much like a miniature copy of Disneyland. I keep having to remind myself we're in the suburbs of Tokyo, where land is astronomically expensive and you can't simply landscape another thousand square kilometers of mosquito-blown Florida swampland for overflow parking whenever you run short of space.

"Did you ever come here as a kid?" I ask.

"Please!" Yoko's glare is one of carefully studied contempt: "I was a Junko Mizuno girl. Hell Babies forever!" Her hand rises in a half-formed fist before she remembers herself and touches her soul-stone instead. "Before. Ahem."

I'm saved from the embarrassment of asking what she means and what the soul-stone has to do with anything when we come to a mosaic-tiled bridge that appears to consist entirely of cake icing. It leads to a pastel-tiled-and-columned lobby like a music hall that's been flashmobbed by a Sylvanian Families convention, at the far end of which we come to the ticket desks. Dr. Suzuki bypasses the queue area and leads me to a desk at one side, where she presents an ID badge to a happy smiling greeter, whose happy smile crumbles away to reveal a stone-faced core of servile obedience. There is a brisk exchange which I don't understand any of except for the deferential body language of our host. We are handed bar-coded staff visitor passes on lanyards. "Wear this at all times," Yoko tells me. "It gives backstage access. Also, access to all rides and attractions is free for official inspectors."

"Right, right." I slip it around my neck and follow her through the turnstile. As we enter, my work phone vibrates. That's odd, because it's just turned four o'clock in the morning back home. I glance at the screen. OFCUT—the occult countermeasures software suite the agency installs on our phones—has thrown up an alert: HIGH THAUM FLUX. The reading makes me wince. A modern smartphone packs more MIPS than a mid-1990s supercomputer, and magic is a side effect of computation, so by executing certain timed operations a phone can function as a kind of thaumaturgic Geiger counter. Right now, if this were a dosimeter and I were in a nuclear establishment, I'd be running away and hunting for the Health and Safety Hotline. "Um, Dr. Suzuki?"

"You *are* warded, yes? Then there is nothing to worry about, as long as we do not linger."

I pinch the bridge of my nose, and force myself not to say anything that might reflect badly on the agency. "Is the soul-stone a ward?"

"Not exactly." She pauses, then relents slightly: "It's a defensive measure. As you can see, I am not entirely human. If attacked, I—my soul—can retreat into the gem."

I am very careful to conceal my expression. Who

am I to throw stones at a Kami walking around in a young woman's vacant body when I'm something similar myself? "Where are we going first?"

"I think . . ." Yoko pulls out her phone, a glittery lilac Sony model that isn't sold outside Japan. "This way." The theme park has a moving map app, helpfully annotated with cute animated animals that squeak excitedly and beckon as they burble pink speech bubbles full of kanji. She leads me past a small food court and an open-fronted store configured like an airport duty-free shop, if duty-free stores sold brightly colored candy and Princess Kitty merchandise to preteen frequent fliers. The kids are, by British standards, unnaturally well-behaved. They wear school uniforms with color-coded caps, and circulate in flocks shepherded by their teachers. By rights they ought to be spinning in circles and bouncing off the ceiling due to the contact sugar high I'm picking up, but discipline is somehow maintained. There is still much squealing and running to and fro, but it's survivable.

Dr. Suzuki decides it's time to clue me in. "There is a camera surveillance office on the second level. I should give you a quick tour of the public space, and then we can go there and I'll show you what we are most worried about."

"The yokai show up on camera?"

For a moment she looks perturbed. "Ordinary yokai don't, but the incursions here are different. They're actual possession cases, eaters that take over the actors playing the Sanrio characters. We exorcise them when we catch them but it's very bad for staff morale. And it can happen to any of them: Cinnamoangels, Bonbonribbon, even Aggretsuko—she caused a lot of trouble, that one! She gets shamelessly drunk and sings death metal, which scares the children. There is also Bad Badtz-Maru, the punk penguin prince. A lot of Sanrio characters are twins or team-ups, so we get multiples. There is swarming behavior, aggression, chanting and food fights, and when Security arrives they attack or flee! These are not teenage pranksters, there is video evidence, and also it happens at random times. We've had visits from non-Sanrio characters too, although they're unable to possess human hosts—there's a pair of escaped Russian mafia rabbit-gangsters and a squad of KGB pandas who chase them. It's really disturbing. And they get more numerous and more aggressive each week. You need to see this."

Yoko leads me through a short tunnel where visitors (mostly children, with a leavening of western tourist goths amidst their Harajuku fashion-victim equivalents) queue for seats in small amusement ride boats. The boats wait to ferry these damned souls across a subterranean river into the Hello Kitty underworld. Being blessed by our park inspector's badges means we go straight to the head of the queue and take our seats. It's much like any other tunnel of love, except for the mouthless cartoon cat presiding over it all—the Saint of Saccharine Sentimentality welcoming us to her domain. The boat sways and yaws and grinds along on rails barely hidden by the water, through a darkened tunnel lined with dioramas showing chubby loveable animal characters in bright primary colors, notably mouthless (or toothless, in those cases where orifices are permitted), frolicking and romping together in wordless joy. My phone constantly vibrates as OFCUT throws up increasingly panicked notifications, like the teletype machine in the control room at Three Mile Island during the reactor meltdown.

"This way to the camera office." I follow Yoko off our ride and into a corridor lined with lovingly curated shrines to dead cartoon idols. We follow a mosaic path that winds artfully between plastic trees with startled faces, then walk through a chintzy bedroom that gives me a strong sense of déjà vu until I realize that it's the original for my hotel room. "Princess

Kitty's bedroom," she says flatly. "Don't linger, it's dangerous."

I shudder. Not only does Princess Kitty lack a mouth with which to scream (should she wish to): judging by the lack of a bathroom, she's also bereft of other orifices. I wonder how she eats or excretes—what powers her metabolism? Does she derive sustenance from stardust and moonshine, or is there something more sinister at work here? Does she feed on the thaum flux generated by massed juvenile adoration, or does she actively parasitize the children's imagination, stealing their individuality and creativity?

We sidle past Princess Kitty's living room and its photo-op couch (the lady herself is currently posing there with a pair of *very* excited eight-year-old members of the Kitty Fan Club, whose parental unit is snapping away at them with a giant Pentax). Next we cross a room with pink-and-orange floor tiles and swagged velvet shades on the light fittings, then walk along a corridor that leads out onto the upper level of a gigantic auditorium. The lower seating levels are mostly full of children and their adult minders, and there appears to be some sort of performance. . . . "Is that a stage play?" I ask in disbelief.

"Not exactly; the Princess Kitty Opera is the highlight of the amusement park, and they repeat it every three hours during opening times." I watch the cast break into song as a horse-drawn pumpkin—a carriage—rolls across the stage, at the head of a column of ballerinas and acrobats, a couple of fire-eating elves, and a baritone in a cartoon dog suit who barks tunefully at the conveyance. Then the lights go down, the baritone falls silent, and a blinding apparition appears overhead. It's Princess Kitty, wearing the most over-the-top frock I've witnessed since the last royal wedding. Her gown blazes with the light of a thousand violet LEDs as she waves her magic wand, sprinkling peace and happiness above the audience. She descends from the rafters on a wire, singing a squeakily enthusiastic aria that I don't need words to know is all about Kitty's joy and harmony. "Here I am, coming to bring peace and love to all mankind," Yoko translates. "There. Ready to go now, please?"

I nod, unable to speak. In my back pocket my phone vibrates again and again, warning me that there may be trouble ahead. I follow Yoko behind the back row of the audience until we come to a blandly featureless door with a sign which I just know for a fact says something like "no admittance, staff only." (The writing may be alien to me, but the design language of liminal spaces is as universal as the tongue of ritual magecraft.)

Dr. Suzuki opens the door to reveal a plain white corridor with scuffed flooring and buzzing overhead fluorescent tubes. There isn't a single smudge of pink in sight. *Phew.* "We are coming to the control room," she explains as we reach a kink in the corridor, beyond which stands another door. This one is guarded by an elderly gent in a blue uniform, white gloves, and peaked cap. He sits atop a high stool beside the entrance, and seems bored to the point of catatonia. I'd take him for a janitor except for the holstered pistol and the rather competent ward he wears around his neck. Ex-military? Ex-cop? I don't get a chance to ask. Dr. Suzuki snaps at him, and he jumps to his feet as quickly as his titanium hip joints permit, then bows stiffly and opens the door for us. Yoko leads me inside—she has a way of making the word *please* sound like an order—and the door closes.

The control room is small and low-ceilinged. It smells of stale cigarette smoke, even though smoking indoors is forbidden. Wall-to-wall desks with cheap PCs face a row of monitors showing ever-switching camera views of the complex. A couple of dudes in short-sleeved shirts and ties face the screens, like a low budget 1960s NASA re-enactment. Periodically one of them mumbles something into his headset mike. It looks like he's playing a first-person shooter on his PC, if you could buy a first-person shooter with the exact same indoor floor plan as Puroland, and all the roving monsters look like lost Japanese kindergarteners. His neighbor is Doc Sleepy, aka Dr. Hasakawa. Today he's very much awake, busily taking notes longhand on some kind of tablet.

"Hello," says Yoko, then she switches to rapid Japanese. Dr. Hasakawa answers her so animatedly that I wonder whether this really *is* Doc Sleepy, or his methhead identical twin. Yoko turns to me and translates: "He says there's nothing new so far today, but the staff are on high alert because there are four more school parties than normal and according to Iko-san the attacks correlate with the number of child visitors—"

I'm distracted by Game Dude's screen. His viewpoint is traveling along a vaguely familiar corridor that after a few seconds I recognize. We walked down it an hour ago. Going by the smoothness of the view, he's actually driving some sort of telepresence robot—we're seeing the view from a mobile camera platform. The kitchen he's heading towards supposedly exists in the magical world of Bunniesfield, which is populated exclusively by pairs of identical-twin rabbits who cook pastries and sweets on a 24/7 basis.

"What's that?" I ask.

"What?" Dr. Suzuki stares at me. I point at Gamer Dude's screen.

"That—"

She leans over Gamer Dude's shoulder and asks him something. He replies. Her back straightens. "Incursion!" she snaps.

I stare at the screen, at a real—if pastel—kitchen, where a pair of cute pink-and-blue bunnies in dresses are carrying mixing bowls. They scurry around the kitchen, bowling children out of the way like tenpins. "It doesn't *look* dangerous—"

The screen flips to a view of a corridor, this time from a ceiling-mounted camera. A black cat with gigantic eyes and whiskers like an old-time TV aerial is loping along. Judging by the terrified visitors scrambling out of his way he's the size of a puma. Then the screen shifts to show a view of the underground river, where a plush white duck in a blue T-shirt is aggressively chasing a boat. "*Fuck*."

Yoko jabs her finger at the screen. "Multiple incursions—it's not a coincidence," she says breathlessly. "It's the big one! It's going critical early! Let's go!" Then she storms towards the door, and I follow.

►◄►◄►◄

As I chase Dr. Suzuki towards the epicenter, trying not to trip over small shouty people in the grip of a sugar-fueled, sticky-fingered ecstasy of animated joy and ignoring the rude looks I receive from their parental units, I reflect that playing live-action *Ghostbusters* is really not my cup of tea.

Yoko is descending towards the lower level, where there's another fake forest, this time with plastic tree trunks and animatronic birdies and small furry things in the undergrowth. "Where are we going?" I ask as I finally catch up with her. For some reason Dr. Hasakawa isn't following us. Indeed, the entire level is curiously short-staffed, and the only visitors I see are a school party that appears to be leaving.

"Head for the shrine!" she calls. "We're nearly there! No time to lose!"

The shrine? Oh, the shrine. *Right.* Because *of course* the beating heart of Puroland wouldn't be the Princess Kitty bedroom suite or the gift store, it'd have to be a faked-up plastic Shinto shrine to Hello Kitty. As we emerge on the bottom level I see it: a rustic house nestling in the branches of an old English oak tree designed by an animator who overdosed on Disney's *Winnie the Pooh* while smoking a botany textbook.

Yoko dashes recklessly out onto the floor of the forest room and I follow her. She rushes towards the wooden staircase that spirals up around the trunk to the tree-house shrine. My phone is going wild: OFCUT reports that the thaum flux here rises with every step I take towards our destination. I can feel mana prickling at the tips of my fingers and toes, and the fine hair at the nape of my neck is standing on end. My defensive ward buzzes like an angry wasp in a nutshell. As we climb, the overhead lights flicker ominously. "Be careful!" I call. "This is a hot zone!" Yoko pushes on. As she steps on the bottom tread her pointy ears take solid form. Both her tails are bushed up, lashing angrily from under the hem of her jacket: "Stop!" I tell her.

"Can't stop," she replies, "it's trying to manifest in the shrine!" Then she hisses like a pressure cooker having a nervous breakdown and leaps three steps higher with a single bound.

I curse as I trail her. "What's so important about the shrine?"

"*Hypocenter*—" For a miracle she pauses for breath. We're on a landing halfway up the tree. My hair stands on end. The tree is the magical equivalent of a van de Graaff generator. If I were an ordinary human I'd be thoroughly creeped out by now: it feels like an entire battalion of black cats are marching over every gravestone in my family tree. "The shrine is the exact center of the park. We're under the entrance hall right now."

Crap crappity-crap and a side order of Ex-Lax. "What *exactly* is the religious significance of the shrine?"

"None whatsoever! At least, not officially." She glances around, thoroughly discomfited by something only a cat lady can sense. "Too many infants come here, and they *adore* Kitty, which amounts to worship—"

"—Got it." To worship is to invoke, to pray is to empower, and praying is basically throwing tiny fragments of soul-stuff at the object of veneration. If Goddess Princess Kitty didn't exist to begin with, she does *now*—Something from beyond the walls of the world has heard the infant prayers, taken on her form, and come to lap daintily at the milky exudate of childish brains. "I thought municipal zoning regulations were supposed to stop this sort of thing?"

"Are you kidding?" She looks at me wildly: "They weren't even keeping mercury out of the shellfish beds back then!"

"Shit. So what happens now?"

"All the yokai that manifest in Puroland try to get to the shrine sooner or later, but I wasn't expecting a spike this big so soon." She leans against the handrail and checks her smartwatch. "The shrine draws them in if they don't mutually annihilate first. Can you stop them?" she asks anxiously.

"Maybe. But why?"

"I need to go upstairs and check the altar for signs of leakage. This is a bad incursion—we saw four yokai, and the thaum field here is still rising. It hasn't nucleated yet but I'm afraid"—she swallows—"this could be the real thing. If they concentrate here they could merge in a power cascade, then reform as a Kaiju."

"But if the Kaiju isn't here yet—"

"It *will* be," she says ominously, fingering her soulstone. "I'll have to force it, to *make* it take a form prematurely. The rest is up to you—keep the yokai away from it, then drain it if you can." She pulls out her phone, hectors someone at the other end of the line, then darts towards the arched entrance over the flight of stairs leading up to the tree house shrine.

The shrine is a tree house made of plastic in the subbasement of a theme park full of weaponized cuteness, harnessed by the juggernaut of the Mammon of Marketing. It should be anticlimactic; a mostly empty four-meter-square room with windows looking out over the pastel-painted forest, a low altar its centerpiece. Except it's not anticlimactic at all.

My skin crawls with a sense of immanent power as I follow Yoko into the room. The altar is familiar from my dream last night, right down to the almost-life-sized statue of Princess Pretty in Pink herself, the goddess of twee. Yoko clearly recognizes it too—and she isn't happy. Her fingernails darken and curve as she extends her claws and tugs at her soul-stone, which is now glowing bright red. Her gait shifts weirdly as she kicks off her shoes and rises on the balls of her feet. It's as if she's wearing a pair of invisible stiletto heels, or her tendons and metatarsals are tightening and lengthening like a cat rising to walk on its toe joints.

All the signs and portents suggest that something ghastly is about to happen. Smears of black tarry goo drip down the walls from ceiling corners where the plastic camera domes have melted. The make-believe sun sets over the plastic grove outside as the artificial light dims towards dusk. Faint sparks of blue-green fire dance along the windowsills. It's St. Elmo's fire: the magic flux is so high that it's causing air ionization, like the radiation over Pripyat after the Chernobyl reactor explosion.

"Wait!" I shout, but I'm not sure Yoko can hear me. A fire alarm is playing deafeningly loud ascending chords, pausing every couple of seconds to play a recording of a woman singing evacuation orders in a high-pitched voice.

I step forward and open my inner eye, prepared to give a brisk psychic beat-down to whatever is causing the statue on the altar to glow an ominous shade of pink—but as I do so, Dr. Suzuki warns me off. "I've got this," she tells me: "I will contain her, then you banish." She reverently places her hands on either side of Princess Pinkness's face and leans forward to kiss the polystyrene idol on the lips.

My phone has been vibrating like a dentist's drill for some minutes. As Yoko's lips touch the statue it emits a wavering howl and crashes, hard. I know this because I'm glancing down at its face when there's a flash of light from the idol so bright that it reflects off the ceiling and walls. For a brain-freezing instant I think of criticality events. But the light isn't the blue of Cerenkov radiation: it's a whiter shade of red. It feels as if we're under attack by a spectral invader, as if the color out of space is pink. A hot flush washes over me and I feel a buzzing sizzle cross my skin as everything around me fades to dreamy pastels—then there's a sharp sting against my breastbone as my ward shatters, and a steel band of oppressively cloying sentimentality clamps tight around my forehead.

I look away from my phone. It's no help right now. The screen has frozen, displaying an upside-down burning goat's skull superimposed over an Elder Sign: the OFCUT alert icon for *you're boned, buddy.* Then the thing occupying Yoko's body straightens up, lets go of the statue, turns to face me, and *smiles.*

I turn and run.

▶ ◀ ▶ ◀ ▶ ◀

The first rule of possessions by higher-order intrusions is *tag you're It.* If it can touch you, you're dead. Or you're It: whichever is worse, there's not much difference.

The second rule of possessions is that they're invariably clumsy and uncoordinated at first, while they grapple with the complexities of managing someone else's body. This looks to be especially true of the Cuteness out of Space, because she seems to be having a seizure. Perhaps Yoko booby-trapped her nervous system? At first, Kitty's stolen avatar is barely capable of standing up. The soul-stone at her throat is so bright it lights up the room, casting cadaverous shadows over her nose and eye sockets as she leans on the devotional statue, clearly unable to balance independently; but her eyes glow with a familiar writhing green luminescence. And her smile? She's all pointy teeth, as if her skin is a caul pulled tight over a very physical gateway to another realm, where something hungers.

So I bolt for the stairs.

I'm not a coward, but I am very much aware that I'm in the basement of a theme park full of children. It takes time to evacuate, even with the fire alarm squeakily pleading for everybody to leave. I can *probably* arm-wrestle Kitty-chan to a draw right now if I Hulk out, but if I do so there will be collateral damage, the kind of collateral you'd expect if some lunatic set off a neutron bomb underneath Disneyworld. (Not to mention rendering Yoko's body uninhabitable by Yoko once she emerges from inside her soul-stone.)

You do not let the Eater of Souls off the leash without casualties ensuing, so brute-forcing a solution is not an option. My first priority must be containment, which means denying Kitty access to handy self-propelled packets of nutrition in the shape of the other yokai, while I try to banish her—

I'm halfway down the stairs when I trip and stumble, twisting as I hit the landing. I end up sprawled on my ass with a white-hot pain whenever I try to move my left ankle. *Shit.* I pull my phone out to find it's finished rebooting, and speed-dial Dr. Hasakawa—*please don't be unconscious.* He answers on the first ring. "Ah, Dr. Howard?"

"Soul-stone," I gasp. With my free hand I grab for the banister rail. "Tell me how it works. Dr. Suzuki is possessed."

"Possessed?" he echoes, and I curse the language barrier, then suddenly realize I'm an idiot. "Neko-Mononoke *has offered her mortal vessel to* Kitty-chan," I say, in a horrible mangling of Japanese and Old Enochian.

"Ah!" A gasp of comprehension is pretty much universal. Doc Sleepy sounds completely awake as he replies, "*Are you certain that Dr. Suzuki has taken on the aspect of the*—" something in Enochian I don't understand, which is unusual "—*and hungers to conquer?*"

"*Yes.*" This isn't an exact translation: Old Enochian is a language better suited for compelling obedience from demonic minions than conversing with colleagues. "*She is in the shrine in the subbasement. I am leaving*—" I'm upright now, and hopping laboriously down the staircase, one bright and shining stab of pain at a time. "*If we can lock her down here I will exorcise her, but you must remove the sacrifices*"—I mean theme park visitors—"*before the apocalypse.*"

"*Thy will be done. Did Neko-Mononoke tell you about her soul-stone? Is it full?*" he asks as I hop down the steps. I'm expending a lot of power fighting off the tendrils of Kitty's will as she tries to sneak into my head, and it's making me *thirsty,* in the horrible soul-parched way that means that the Eater of Souls is awake and eager to feed. (It's a timely reminder that I, too, am merely a mortal vessel for something unnatural that hungers for human sustenance. Kyonshī, hopping vampires, are a thing of legend in this part of the world. There's enough irony in my situation that a skilled blacksmith could turn it into a katana.)

"Her soul-stone—" I pause for air. *"It's glowing pink. Is that right?"*

"Yes!"

"I will starve the fire of fuel: the rest is up to you." He ends the call.

I'm nearly at the bottom step when I hear thuds and banging from above as Zombie Hello Kitty staggers slowly downstairs. Her presence seems to suck all the blues and greens out of the room. The forest is turning into a washed-out murdervista, more Martian invasion than extradimensional incursion.

I limp out across the tiled floor. It should be green, but in Kitty Hell it's the horrible greyish red of an undercooked steak. I only make it halfway to the entrance before the door opens and a series of nightmare playmates prance in. A full-scale multiple incursion is clearly in progress, in the shape of the corrupted nightmares of the Sanrio art department rather than classic yokai. Here comes a lazy anthropomorphized egg yolk on a self-propelled albumin-colored sofa pushed by a human-sized pink rabbit wearing bows on her head, ears, and paws. (She'd be cute if her incisors weren't ivory chisels the length of my forearm.) They're followed closely by a gothic Lolita bat-girl, a crazed punk penguin with a green brush-cut and a biker jacket, and a green furry spider-thing with writhing tentacles that clearly originated somewhere far outside the cute-osphere but decided to crash the party anyway. Before the incursion they were human actors in cartoon animal suits. Now their eyes are glowing, and I can feel their malice from clear across the forest floor. They heft improvised weapons (a fire extinguisher, a bike chain, a janitor's broom), and they spread out to surround me.

I need to buy time, so I limp away as fast as I can, heading for the opposite wall where—*yes*—there is another unmarked "no admittance, staff only" door, because *of course* there has to be discreet access for cleaners in all the public areas.

I go to my knees in front of the door and dump my pocket lint on the ground. This is the stuff it always has in its pocketses: phone, plastic baggie half-full of grey-green powder, multitool, Oyster card (because London), and assorted junk I forgot to offload. I always carry a conductive-ink pen, let's hope it hasn't run dry. I use it to draw a wide half circle across the floor before me to shape an absolutely minimal containment grid, then pull out my lucky USB cable. It ends in two leads which I tape to the terminal nodes sketched on the summoning circuit diagram. The other end plugs straight into the socket on the bottom of my phone, and I fire up a different app in the OFCUT suite.

With my inner eye open I watch the yokai-possessed bodies lurch across the room towards me. They're still working on their muscle control, which is good news. Seen by soul-glow they're fluorescent, glowing the unhealthy-for-mammals green of luminous fungi digesting their host cadavers. Behind them the tree house and staircase glow ever-brighter, tall aurora-like curtains of light dancing across them. A mana-source so bright that it lights up the entire hall slowly descends, for She Who Cannot Scream is coming.

I think fast: *Normal yokai emerge as virtual particle pairs from an excited background magic field. Before she let the Kitty-thing in, Yoko was entangled with a kami, not unlike my own situation. And she had a bolt-hole.* Hmm. *Must be cramped in there. I wonder who's the bigger hungry ghost—Princess Kitty, or the Eater of Souls?*

I can't let the thing wearing Yoko's body eat its way through the Sanrio pantheon before I get her, because with each one she consumes—or each pair she mutually annihilates—she'll get bigger. So I've got to get them out of the way first.

Nerving myself, I straighten up, testing my bad ankle to see if it will take my weight. The answer is definitely-maybe, going by the bright and shiny nail of pain stabbing through my ankle joint. I can stand, but if I try to run, or do much more than a painful shuffle, it could give way under me. So I palm my pen and tug the door open behind me.

The herd of yokai charge, very slowly, as I make my move. Cats meow, puppies yip excitedly, the penguin quacks like a Japanese Bart Simpson. I limp backward through the doorway, then slam it shut as the egg yolk on the pink chaise hurls itself at the ward on the floor. I hear an angry sizzle and a screech of pain. The ward is working, but it won't keep them out for long. However, I don't *need* long.

I concentrate on the back of the door and begin to sketch a much more creative ward, by the flickering light of the fire alarm on the ceiling.

There is a trick to using the ghost roads, or the other virtual passageways that tunnel behind the cracks and crevices of reality, such as hotelspace. First, you need to know that they're there and that it's possible to traverse them. Second, you need to be able to link to both your entrypoint and your destination, lest you become disoriented and wander forever in a manifold of white-painted cinder-block walls and exposed ductwork—at least until the Hounds sense your presence and hunt you down. (Sudden Death Jeopardy adds a certain frisson to applied graph theory.) Finally, you need enough magic to open the way in the first place—which is what stops most people, but not me.

I draw an eternal golden braid on the back of the door, then *push*. Power bleeds through my diagram, glowing and leaving me lightheaded and weak. Then, before the yokai on the other side can breach the ward, I pull the door open and step back out to confront them.

As I pass the threshold my eyes cross and I feel very strange. Nothing is quite where it should be: my right ankle is a brilliant crack of pain whenever I put my weight on it, I'm slightly dizzy, and the spiral staircase in the base of the tree house corkscrews the wrong way. But the gang of yokai aren't here anymore: the floor is empty except for a badly smudged ward and my phone. I stoop to pick it up and the display is unreadable, mirrored right to left. *It worked,* I realize, too drained to feel triumphant. I scoop up the items I need and limp back towards the tree.

What I'm attempting to do is quite dangerous. No, scratch that: it's *extremely* dangerous, and if I don't reverse it—assuming I'm not eaten in the next few minutes by the Pale Puce Peril—I'll die. I could starve to death on a diet of perfectly ordinary food in this mirror-world: every peptide bond and saccharide, every biomolecule in my body has had its rotational symmetry reversed, because I sketched a Möbius ward on a ghost road door then stepped back through it. I am where I started, but I'm here as my looking-glass self. I scratch my chin—it feels oddly unfair that I haven't spontaneously sprouted an evil-me goatee—then limp onwards.

The yokai are still here in a manner of speaking. When I opened the door they rushed through, twisted right out of this universe and into a symmetry-reversed mirror of the ghost roads of Puroland. I can feel them battering at the ward, trying to get back in. But they're locked out until they can break down the door, which buys me time to deal with their boss.

She's waiting for me at the bottom of the staircase, fur bristling and ears flattened back, hissing and ready for blood.

"*Hello, Kitty,*" I say in Old Enochian, and smile at her.

"*You!*" Kitty snarls at me, extending her claws. "*What have you done to my food?*"

She's made some changes since she moved into her new host body. For Dr. Suzuki's sake I hope they're reversible. Her head is now outsized and round, the pale kawaii moon-face of Princess Kitty overlaid on a biological scaffold of muscle, bone, and gristle. Everything around us is suffused with a pinkish penumbra of peace and joy. I can hear it whispering at the edges of my mind: *Accept my love and everything will be happy forever.* Luckily the soul-stone is still bound securely around her throat, ignored or forgotten.

"I locked them outside," I tell her, gesturing at the door. Her eyes track my hand so she doesn't notice me palming a small baggie in the other. "If you want them back you'll have to get past me."

The kami's bushed-up tail lashes angrily. Her fur is standing on end, and her pupils are blown. I have a cat (it moved in with us and demanded service; Mo currently has custody), and I know enough to read her body language: Kitty is preparing to pounce. "*Hungry! Eat you first! Prepare to die!*"

She gapes wide, which gives me a good look at the ridged palate and fangs of a medium raptor. And that's when I throw the baggie of catnip in her mouth—the half of it I didn't use on the Neko-mata at the cat café.

Nepetalactone, the essential oil that's the active

ingredient in catnip, is something to which Princess
Kitty has had zero exposure, because the denizens of
Puroland are squeaky-clean avatars of childhood in-
nocence who don't do drugs. Her reaction to getting
a gobful of the powdered herb is spectacular: First her
mouth closes. Then it sags open as she takes a drunken
step forward. Then her eyes cross, and she sneezes con-
vulsively as she falls to her knees and rolls on her side.

I squat painfully beside her. The soul-stone is glowing, so there's still hope for Yoko if I can eat the in-
truder's soul. As I'm round the Möbius twist, my own
occupant is in fact chirally opposed to the hungry
ghost in her—only, the Eater of Souls is bigger and
more powerful than the poor starving cat goddess. So
I lean close and open my lips and . . .

Reader, I do *not* kiss the foreign liaison officer.
That would be workplace harassment, gross professional misconduct, and besides *ew*. (Also, I'm married.) But the thing I carry inside my head spreads
its jaws wide as I lean close to the anti-thing wearing
Dr. Suzuki's meat suit, and it wraps its barbed suckers
around Kitty's soul, sinks stingers into her abdomen,
and pumps metaphysical venom into her heart. There
is a great and terrible scream from the altar in the tree

house as something rips itself free of my mind and spins me round, right round—

►◄►◄►◄

And I come to lying on the floor beside Dr. Suzuki's body. Everything hurts. At first all I can see is shades of grey, but her soul-stone is pulsing, which I fuzzily realize is a good sign. I feel as if I've been beaten with cricket bats, and I am *full,* my metaphysical stomach stuffed to bursting. I'm not sure I could banish Tinkerbell right now, much less another yokai. I also feel oddly bereft, as if a source of goodness and virtue has been sucked out of the world. (It's actually a camouflage mechanism, something Kitty developed in order to convince her victims she's all sweetness and light: cuteness is an effective predation strategy for monsters.)

I force myself to sit up then swear when I bash my left ankle, the one I injured on the stairs. Next I check Dr. Suzuki. She's breathing, which is another good sign: I roll her into the recovery position and limp over to the "staff only" door.

The ward I drew there is already smudged. I smear

it some more until I finally manage to break the line. Then I pull the door open. The yokai have disappeared from sight down a curving, grey-walled tunnel, and the Möbius loop on the back of the door is intact. Good thing it was behind them when they rushed through; if they'd seen it, I'd be in trouble. Sacred geometry is problematic, especially the non-Euclidian variety, but I step across the threshold once more—careful to keep the door open—then start amending the diagram on the door.

Möbius strips have some fascinating topological properties. For starters, they're a two-dimensional object embedded in a three-dimensional space. What I've sketched isn't actually three-dimensional—of necessity, it's a 2D projection of a 3D object. Nevertheless I amend it, cutting along the middle of the strip, and as I cut my head begins to ache. It's hard to keep going but I persist until I find myself staring cross-eyed at a continuous band with *two* twists in it—at which point I cautiously step back across the threshold and close the door behind me.

Maybe the lost yokai will find their way home from the mirror continuum, but it will almost certainly take them a very long time indeed—long enough for us to get a rescue party ready to deal with them. In the meantime, I stumble over to Dr. Suzuki and sink down beside her, then wait for the security team to arrive. The fire alarm abruptly stops, leaving my ears ringing in the silence. My phone vibrates with an incoming notification. I look at the screen, register the date, and swear quietly.

The job isn't finished yet. Kitty is drained for now, deprived of sustenance and too weak to go full Kaiju and love-bomb Tokyo, but it's not over until we can rebuild the containment ward under the goddamn tree house. Not to mention locking down the ghost roads leading to the altar, such as the corridor I just twisted right out of reality and into a pocket mirror-universe. But I've bought us some time. It'll have to be enough for now.

Once we get this mess cleaned up I am going to fly straight home and sleep for a week. Forget sightseeing, I'm burned out. I'll figure out a way to take some time off work and make it up to Mo. We're due some quality time together after all, and I'm not going to let *anything* get in the way of that.

► ◄ ► ◄ ►

(Bob's story is continued in The Delirium Brief*)*

ACKNOWLEDGMENTS

This wasn't my idea originally! So I want to credit my wife for insisting I take her to Puroland for her birthday after the 2007 World Science Fiction Convention, then asking the obvious question: "What if 'The Colour Out of Space' was pink?"